LONG RUN

JOSEPH BRUCHAC

7th Generation

SUMMERTOWN, TENNESSEE

Library of Congress Cataloging-in-Publication Data is available upon request.

7th Generation
an imprint of Book Publishing Company
PO Box 99, Summertown, TN 38483
888-260-8458
bookpubco.com
nativevoicesbooks.com

ISBN: 978-1-93905-309-1

21 20 19 18 17 16   1 2 3 4 5 6 7 8 9

BookPublishing Co.

Book Publishing Company is a member of Green Press Initiative. We chose to print this title on paper with 100% postconsumer recycled content, processed without chlorine, which saved the following natural resources:

- 21 trees
- 658 pounds of solid waste
- 9,823 gallons of water
- 1,811 pounds of greenhouse gases
- 9.75 million BTU of energy

For more information on Green Press Initiative, visit www.greenpressinitiative.org. Environmental impact estimates were made using the Environmental Defense Fund Paper Calculator. For more information visit www.papercalculator.org.

CONTENTS

Seattle

Travis Hawk stared toward the bay.

"I want to run," he said.

His voice was soft, and no one heard him.

He stood in the downstairs doorway. It was early. The street was quiet. No one else was up yet. He'd been planning to run. Run down and up the hills. Run with the salt air in his face. Run with the wind at his back. Run, run, his feet striking the ground like the soft beat of a drum.

Running was one thing he was good at doing. Travis had long legs. He was only seventeen, but his chest was broader than the chests of many men. That made space for his lungs. He could run for miles and not gasp for breath.

"Young man, you were born for this." That was what the cross-country coach had said, trying to get Travis to join the team. But Travis couldn't do that.

"I have to go home after school," he told the coach.

When he said that, it made him sad. It wasn't true because of one word. That word was "home." He didn't have a home.

Travis lived in a homeless shelter with his father. His mother had died when Travis was twelve. His father had been on his way home from Iraq when it happened. She died from something called meningitis. Travis hated that word "meningitis." Hearing it reminded him of two things. The first was his mother's sudden death. She was healthy one day and then gone three days later. The second thing the word reminded him of was his father's anger.

"Meningitis!" It was the first thing his father said when Travis saw him at the funeral. He said it like a curse word.

His father kept saying that word. The more he drank, the louder he said it. He shouted it at Travis and at Grandma Kailin and Grampa Tomah.

His father was a skilled carpenter. But there were no jobs for him in Maine.

"Travis can stay with us," Grampa Tomah had said.

"I'm his father. He needs to be with me. I can take care of him. I can get work anywhere."

But anywhere turned out to be everywhere. They went wherever there was work. Or wherever there *might* be work. Over the last four years his father had worked in ten different states. And wherever he went, Travis went with him.

"You need me," his father said. "And I need you."

That was why Travis could not do cross-country running. He couldn't stay after school. He had to go home as soon as school was over. His father expected that. Even if he was not yet back at the shelter, Rick Hawk expected Travis to be there waiting for him.

The only free time Travis ever had was early morning. That was when he could run.

But not today. It was raining too hard. He only had one pair of shoes. Good running shoes. Secondhand, but almost new. The only nice thing his father ever got him. Travis didn't want them to get soaked.

Rain. That was nothing new.

"It's Seattle," Travis thought. "It's a city named for a dead Indian. What else should anyone expect here?"

"It rains here a lot," his father had said when they arrived in the city. Then his father had made a joke. "If you live here long enough, you grow gills like a fish."

"Or you start to drink like a fish," Travis thought.

His father was still asleep. He hadn't moved since he fell into bed late last night. Travis had checked to make sure he was still breathing. He wasn't dead. He was just drunk. A drunk Indian.

"I will never get drunk," Travis thought.

The homeless shelter was on a hill. Everything in Seattle was on a hill. Travis looked toward the bay. He couldn't see it. The rain was too heavy. But he could smell the bay. He could hear the cries of gulls and the WHOOOONK of the foghorn on the ferryboat.

Mount Rainier was out there on the other side of the bay. But Travis couldn't see Mount Rainier either.

"Just wait," his father had said. "You'll see it."

It was the same way his father talked about getting work.

"Just wait," Rick Hawk would say. "I'll get a good job here. I've been in Seattle before. I know my way around. I used to work here years ago. I have friends here."

He had found some of those friends. Lenny Black was one of them. Lenny was a construction worker like Rick Hawk. They had met while working on a job together the first time Rick lived in Seattle. Lenny's wife was named Lenore. L and L. That was what they called themselves. They were both ten years older than Travis's father. They had round, friendly faces. Lenore was over six feet tall and Lenny was even taller. He had to duck his head when he walked under a doorway. They were both from the Colville Reservation. They had saved up and bought a two-story house in the east end of Seattle.

Rick and Travis stayed at Lenny and Lenore's house at first. Their house was not big, but lots of people stayed there. Some just visited for a night. Some stayed for weeks at a time. All of them were Indian. L and L's Free Hotel—

that's what everyone called Lenny and Lenore's house.

"The economy is down now," his father had said. "It has to pick up. There's always a job for a good carpenter."

But he did not find a job. He did find some other friends. They went drinking together. At first it was just on Saturday nights. Then it was every night.

Travis liked it at Lenny and Lenore's. They never drank anything except water.

Every night at dinner Lenny would do the same thing. Before they ate he would hold up a full glass of water.

"This is one of the best gifts the Creator gave us," Lenny always said.

Neither Lenny or Lenore ever spoke a harsh word to anyone. But Travis and Rick had to leave. One night in February, Travis's father came in late. He smelled of alcohol. His hair was wet from the rain. There were bruises on his face. He looked like an angry grizzly bear.

"They threw me out of the bar," he growled. His voice was thick from drinking. "After all the business I gave them!"

His eyes were half closed as he spoke. Travis knew what was going to come next.

"No, Dad," he said. "No!"

His father ignored him. He picked up a plate from the dish drainer. He lifted it up and smashed it on the floor.

Travis held out his hand. "Dad," Travis said, "that's not our stuff. Please stop."

His father grabbed his arm. He pushed him out of the room and threw him onto the floor.

Travis wasn't hurt much. He knew how to fall.

His father went back into the kitchen. He kept breaking things. Cups, glasses, plates. Travis just sat on the floor. Blood was dripping from his lip. His father's elbow had struck him there. He knew his father didn't mean to do that, but it still hurt.

Lenny came downstairs. He reached out and helped Travis to his feet. He used a tissue to wipe the blood off Travis's lip. Someone put an arm around Travis and squeezed his shoulders. It was Lenore.

Lenny went to the kitchen door. He didn't go into the kitchen.

"Brother," Lenny said. He didn't shout. He just spoke that one quiet word, "brother."

Rick Hawk looked at them. He looked at the plate in his hand. He stared at it as if he had never seen a plate before. Then he put it down gently on the kitchen table. He turned and walked out the door into the cold rain. He did not come back till the next afternoon. Travis had already packed their bags.

"You don't have to leave," Lenny said.

"Yes, we do," Rick Hawk replied. He gave Lenny a handful of dollar bills.

"For what I broke," he said.

Lenny took the money and shoved it into his shirt pocket.

Lenore hugged Travis hard. "Take care of your father," she whispered to him.

"I can't," Travis thought. But he nodded anyway.

They moved first into a one-room apartment in a building that smelled like burned grease. The bathroom was down the hall. The shower was broken.

"This shower is just like me," his father joked. "It don't work."

It was all they could afford. They only stayed there for two months and then the money ran out. They had to leave the apartment and go to the first shelter.

The people who ran the shelter meant well. Seattle was proud of its homeless shelters. They kept them clean and gave people decent food. They had training programs to help people find work. They even had special shelters for homeless young people who didn't have parents with them. Travis wondered if he would have been happier at one of those shelters. Probably not.

The shelter they were in now was their second one. The first one had been on the other side of town.

When they arrived at that first shelter, Travis made a friend. His name was Will Chan. He was the same age as Travis. He was in the shelter with his father too.

Will and his father had been homeless for five years. But Will was not depressed. His father had a hard time finding a job, but he didn't drink a lot.

"My dad just likes to travel," Will said. "He used to be some sort of hippie. He likes it on the road. I guess I do, too. It's like we are wandering monks from the old days in China, fighting evil landlords and saving pretty girls."

Will smiled as he said that.

Will was always smiling. He gave Travis a nickname: Brother Hawk. Travis liked the sound of it. Will told Travis about things he had learned from being homeless.

"It's not bad, Brother Hawk," he said. "Take food, for example. You can always find food in the city. You check out the bins behind the grocery stores. Every night they throw out tons of stuff. Or go to the dumpsters behind the best restaurants." Will chuckled, and his face creased into a big smile. "Man, you would not believe what people leave on their plates. And you can sleep pretty good in a cardboard box. It doesn't need to be that big. Smaller ones stay warmer. And bad weather is no problem. Just put plastic bags over the top. Then it doesn't get soaked in the rain."

Will also had a book about survival.

"Check this out, Brother Hawk."

It was the coolest book Travis ever saw. Will loaned it to Travis. Travis read it from cover to cover three times. It talked about everything. It told how to survive on your own in the forest and in the city.

"We can go camping sometime," Will said. "We'll take nothing with us but a blanket and a knife. We'll build shelters like those in the book. We'll live off the land."

That never happened. Will and his father left soon after Travis arrived.

Will had the survival book in his hand when they said goodbye.

"I thought about giving this to you," Will said. He wasn't smiling.

Travis shook his head. "No," he said. "You keep it." He tapped his head. "I've got it all in here."

Will smiled then. "Brother Hawk, you are one cool dude."

They slapped palms and fist-bumped.

"Stay strong, my friend," Will said.

"You too."

A week later, Travis and his father had to move. Rick Hawk didn't tell him why. It just happened. One day they were in the shelter near the east side. The next day they were up on the hill on the other side of the town.

*　　*　　*

Travis looked out again at the foggy bay. They had been in Seattle for six months. They had arrived in November. Now it was almost June. All that time the mountain had been hidden by clouds.

Travis knew a lot about Mount Rainier. He hadn't learned it at school. He had read it on his phone. He knew how tall it was. He knew why it was called Mount Rainier. He knew its Native name. Its Native name was Tahoma. He had even found a story about the mountain told by Chief Seattle's people. They said the mountain was alive. A fire spirit lived inside it. One day that spirit would wake up. That spirit did not like it when people climbed the mountain.

What would it be like to climb Mount Rainier? His father had climbed Mount Rainier before Travis was born. He had told Travis about that climb.

It had taken Rick Hawk two days to make the climb. All he had with him was a small backpack with a sleeping bag. He had carried a pouch of tobacco that was a gift for the mountain. It was cloudy as he climbed. It was cloudy when he made his camp for the night. It was still cloudy the next day. When he reached the top, the wind swept away the clouds. He could see for miles. He saw all of Puget Sound. He saw the mountains all around.

"It was wonderful," his father had said. "I felt as if I was in the sky land."

Then he told Travis a story.

"Long ago," Rick Hawk said, "the sky land was close to the earth. That was before this city was here. Back then the animals and people all lived together. They shared everything. The sky land was so close that the people and animals could just jump up into it. There was lots of food up there. There were lakes and streams. The sun was always shining, and it was always warm. It was beautiful up there in the sky land."

Rick Hawk had been smiling when he told the story. It made Travis feel good to see his father smile. When his dad wasn't drinking, he was the greatest father.

"Someday," Rick said, "you and I will climb that mountain."

Travis almost believed it.

Someday. Rick Hawk often said that. Someday.

Someday was never today.

Travis had never climbed a mountain.

His father had been the same age as Travis when he first climbed a mountain. He'd climbed it with Grampa Tomah. That mountain was called Ktaahdin. It was the biggest mountain in Maine. But that was years ago.

Grampa Tomah was too old now to climb mountains. Maine, where he lived, was three thousand miles away. Travis had lived there with his dad when Travis was little. After Mom died.

"Someday," Rick Hawk would tell Travis, "we'll go back there. We'll go see your grandparents again. Someday."

Someday.

Travis knew that "someday" actually meant never. Rick Hawk would never take Travis to

see Grampa Tomah and Grandma Kailin. He'd
never take Travis mountain climbing. The only
thing Rick Hawk climbed now were the stairs in
the shelter. And that was usually late at night.
He stumbled up those stairs as he climbed. Like
last night.

"Travis," he had called, his voice slurred.
"Travis, come help me."

Travis had helped him. When they got to
their room, his father pushed him into the wall.
Then he punched him in the stomach. Rick
Hawk was like that when he was drunk. He hit
people. Hard.

He also said things he didn't mean when he
was drunk.

"You are useless, kid. Useless," he had said.
"Why do I have to take care of you? You just
hold me back. Useless."

Travis put his hand on his stomach. He felt
the bruise there. But what his father had said
hurt more.

Useless.

*I'm not useless. I can run. That's one thing I
can do.*

Travis looked out the doorway. The rain had
finally stopped. But the fog had become thick.
All he could see was the fog. His eyes were wet
from the mist.

Pike Place Market was somewhere down there. People were down there doing things. People were always doing things in Seattle, even when it was cool and rainy. They were real people with real lives. Travis wished he was one of them.

"I'm tired of being afraid," Travis said. He said it softly to himself.

Then he shook his head. No, that wasn't it. It wasn't about being afraid. He was tired of always expecting things to be the way they were.

"I can't stay here," Travis thought. The thought surprised him. "But how can I leave my father?"

Then another thought hit him. It hit him harder than his father's drunken fists.

I have to leave. I have to run. Not tomorrow. Now!

Reasons

Travis looked at his sleeping father. His face was peaceful. Rick Hawk never looked angry when he was sleeping.

"I love you, Dad," Travis whispered. He thought for a moment about kissing his father on the forehead. He knew his father loved him, even though he never said it. But his father might wake up if he kissed him. Then he would stop Travis from going.

"I'll never let you go." That was what his father had said many times. "You are all I got left."

It always confused Travis when his father said that. How could his dad tell him he was worthless and then say that?

"I can't help you," Travis thought. "I have to help myself."

He'd thought before about what he would do when he turned eighteen. At eighteen he was legally an adult. Then he could get away. Maybe go live with his grandparents. Maybe join the Marines. His father couldn't stop him then. But he was still seventeen. Still a minor. His birthday was three months away.

Travis crept down the stairs. It was too early for anyone else to be up, but he still had to be quiet. His father wasn't the only reason he had to run. When he reached the door, he slung his backpack over his shoulder.

The other reason he had to run had been hidden in his pack.

"Evan," he thought. "It had to be Evan who put that stuff in there. Evan and Mannie." Who else would try to set him up? They were the ones who hated him.

What was it that his father said sometimes? When he was sober and acting like a real dad?

"It only takes a minute to make a friend for life."

Travis nodded. That had been true with Will Chan. But it took even less time than that to make an enemy. Two enemies.

Evan Black was the first one. He was the same age as Travis but much shorter and skinny as a stick. Mannie Senter was the second one. He was taller than Travis and built like a pear. He had narrow shoulders, pitted cheeks, and a big stomach. He and Evan were always together.

Travis knew why they hated him. The first reason was because he was Native. There were always people who didn't like you because of that, and Evan and Mannie were among them. Whenever they said anything about Indians, it was always nasty.

"Indians are all on welfare."

"Indians are all alcoholics."

"You can't trust Indians."

"Indians steal."

"Indians stink."

"Indians suck."

The second reason the two boys were out to get him was more important. He wouldn't do what they wanted him to do. Travis looked older than seventeen. The other two boys looked young for their age.

The first day Travis was at the shelter, they came up to him.

The skinny kid with long, straw-blond hair leaned close. Travis read the words on his black T-shirt: "I CUT DOWN TREE HUGGERS."

"Indian, right?" the boy said.

Travis said nothing.

He poked Travis in the chest with one finger.

"Want to get along here?" the boy asked. His voice was a harsh whisper.

Travis still didn't say anything.

The blond boy gestured to the big, heavy-shouldered boy with him.

"Mannie here will help you understand. Tell him the facts of life, Senter."

"You bet, Black."

Mannie Senter stepped forward. His stomach stuck out like a basketball. He bumped Travis with his belly. Travis stepped back.

"Hey, Indian? You hear what my buddy Evan said?"

Travis nodded.

Evan held out a crumpled ten-dollar bill.

"You take this and buy us a six-pack of beer. The Asian guy at the corner store won't even check your ID."

Travis shook his head. He turned and went back into the room that been assigned to him and his father.

"Bad move, man," Evan hissed.

"You just failed the test. Big time," Mannie said.

Travis wasn't afraid of them. The only person Travis feared was his father. And that was only when his father was drinking.

Travis knew some karate. Not much, but enough. He had taken lessons when he was fifteen. They were living in New Hampshire then. His father had a good job building a power plant. He had enough money to send Travis to a self-defense school.

"You need to build up those muscles," Rick Hawk had said. "Don't let no one push you around."

He signed Travis up at a kenpō karate school in Portsmouth.

To Travis's surprise, he enjoyed the classes. He went three times a week after school. He never missed a class.

Master Kwan was the sensei, the teacher at the school. After Travis had been there for four months, Master Kwan took him aside.

"Good balance. Strong base. You are a natural. Stay with me three years and you'll have your black belt."

Travis had smiled. But it was a brief smile. He'd heard stuff like that before. He'd always been told that he had a natural talent for this or that. Someone was willing to teach him. All he needed was time to develop it.

"Time," Travis had thought back then. "I'll never have that."

And, as always, he was right.

Rick Hawk was laid off the day after Master Kwan had said that. Two days later, Travis and his father were on a bus to Oklahoma.

"A bus," Travis thought. "That's the way to start."

Hitching was too slow. He might get caught. He also didn't want to stand out in the rain. He wanted to get away from it all as fast as he could. Away from the shelter. Away from his father. Away from the rain.

Travis knew where the bus station was. That was the way they had come into Seattle. The station was two miles from the shelter. An easy run.

He already knew the bus schedule. He'd looked it up on his phone two days ago. He knew the time for the next bus going due east. It would leave at 6:46 a.m.

He heard a sound from behind him.

Was it his father? Evan or Mannie?

He spun around.

No one was there. It was just the creaking of the building. The shelter was an old building. It was always making noises. The groaning sound was coming from somewhere in its foundation. It sounded like a ghost moaning, "Goooo awaaaay."

Even the building knows I have to leave.

No one was up yet. Evan and Mannie never left their rooms till breakfast.

His dad was not awake. Rick Hawk would sleep until noon, maybe later. He had been very drunk. It took time for him to sleep it off.

Travis mentally ran through the list of things in his backpack. His wallet with his ID. The $82 he'd managed to hide from his father. It was money he had earned from doing yard work for people. If he stuck around, he could earn even more. The school year was over. He had more time to work.

He shook his head. If he didn't leave, he'd end up with no money at all. His father would take it. Plus there was Evan and Mannie.

They wouldn't stop trying to cause trouble. If he stayed, he'd have to fight them.

The best way to fight your enemies is by not fighting. Master Kwan had told him that.

Travis continued his mental list. No cell phone. He'd heard you could be tracked through a cell phone, so he would leave it behind. Two clean red T-shirts with nothing written on them. Two sets of underclothes. A second pair of Levis. Two pairs of socks. One toothbrush and half a tube of toothpaste. A plastic bag with a space blanket in it. The deerskin leather pouch holding the fire-making kit Grampa Tomah had given him.

"A man who knows how to make a shelter and a fire," Grampa Tomah had told him, "can survive just about anywhere."

And one black lock-blade knife.

Travis bought the knife three years ago when they lived in Maine. He had used the Christmas money his grandparents had given him.

"Get something you can use," Grampa Tomah had whispered. "A good knife, maybe. That is all you need in the woods. Just a knife. Get it before your father knows you have this money."

The plastic bag with the crack cocaine in it was no longer in his backpack. It was now in the room Evan shared with his father. Evan's father hadn't been there when Travis went in. He was working the night shift at a convenience store. Travis had placed the bag under Evan's cot. Evan hadn't woken up because Travis knew how to move quietly. He knew how to move like a bear through the forest. He'd learned that from his grandfather.

The police could be arriving soon. And they'd likely be told that the long-haired Indian kid in the shelter had drugs. Tipped off by Evan or

Mannie. But there would be no drugs in Travis's room. Just his father, still drunk. So drunk they probably wouldn't be able to wake him up.

Travis thought for a moment about that. Would his father get in trouble? No. It wasn't illegal to be an alcoholic.

It was illegal to be a minor and on your own, though. Three months till he turned eighteen. Then he'd be on his own legally. But not now.

No way he would wait for three months.

Time to go. Now!

He turned and looked east. The only people in the world who loved him were there. His grandparents.

Even if he had a phone, he couldn't call them. They lived in the woods. They had no cell phone. No TV. Just a battery-powered radio. And they had Grampa Tomah's old Jeep to use if they needed to go to the town of Eagle Lake for supplies.

"We will know when you are thinking about us," Grandma Kailin had told Travis. Her voice was as sweet as a wood thrush singing. Remembering her voice made Travis smile.

Travis thought about his grandparents. He tried to send his thoughts to them.

I am coming to you.

He shut the door of the shelter behind him. He stepped out into the fog. He began to run.

The Bus

Travis climbed the steps into the bus. It was only half full. He moved down the aisle and found a seat four rows from the back.

It was a good place to sit.

Don't ever take the seat furthest back. It's too close to the bathroom. You don't want to smell that for a hundred miles.

Don't take the seat in front behind the driver. Whenever people get on, you'll be the first person they see.

He had learned that from his father.

He didn't want to be seen. He wanted to be invisible. He wanted to disappear. He didn't want anyone to know where he was going. Especially his father.

Would his father come looking for him? Maybe not. He didn't act as if he cared about Travis. All he cared about now was getting drunk.

Did he want his father to come looking for him? Travis wasn't sure. The only thing he was sure about was that he had to go.

The wall outside his window began to move. No, *they* were moving. The bus was backing up.

Next stop would be Spokane. That was far enough to start with.

He kept looking out the window. He was so tired. It had been a long time since he had slept a whole night. The bus went up and down the hills. Its motor sounded like a huge cat purring.

Soon there was water on both sides of the road. Then there was a sign for Puyallup, then Tacoma, then Auburn. A large sign for I-90 appeared on the right.

Beyond that sign was a big old cedar tree. It had two limbs that lifted up like arms. Its bark was dark brown. Its needles were as green as new grass. It made Travis think of a story Grandma

Kailin had told him. Years ago his grandparents had been traveling cross-country. They used to make trips like that all the time to see friends. At the top of a long hill, the brakes gave out on their old car. They could not stop. The car kept going faster and faster. It seemed as if they were going to crash.

"There was an old cedar by the road," Grandma Kailin had said. "Cedar trees have always been our friends. I asked that tree to help us. As soon as I said that, our brakes started working again."

Grandma Kailin had smiled and nodded. "Every year, whenever we traveled, we would stop at that tree. We would say thanks to it for helping us."

Travis watched the cedar tree until it was lost from sight.

"Grandfather Cedar," he whispered. "Help me as I travel."

He wrapped his arms around his backpack and closed his eyes.

*   *   *

"You okay, son?"

Travis woke up. He lifted one hand in front of his face as if to protect himself. A man was looking down at him. The man's skin was as dark as cedar bark. He'd never seen this man before, but the man's broad face looked kind.

"You speak English, son?" The man's voice was deep and pleasant.

Travis nodded.

"Right," the man said. There was a smile on his face now. "I was just joking. I know you speak English. You were talking in your sleep."

"What did I say?" Travis asked.

"Nothing much. Just that you had to run. Mind if I sit down?"

Travis nodded again.

The man slid down into the seat beside him. He held out his hand.

"Diggs is the name. Poems are my game. Lawrence Diggs."

Travis took the hand of Lawrence Diggs. He didn't squeeze his hand. He just held it lightly for a moment. That was how he had been taught to shake hands.

Lawrence Diggs nodded. "Indian handshake," he said. "Good for you. No need to try to break a man's hand like some folks do. Mind telling me your name?"

"Travis, sir."

Lawrence Diggs settled back in his seat and crossed his arms. He looked over his shoulder at Travis.

"Where you off to, Travis?"

"East."

Lawrence Diggs chuckled. "Travis the traveler, off to the east. Traversing the land to see what he can see. Now me, I am just going to Spokane. Going to see my grandson, name of Dan." He patted his breast pocket. "Tomorrow's his seventh birthday. What I have here is a poem. One I wrote just for him."

Travis looked out the window. Big fir and pine trees were whizzing by. Mountains with snow on their peaks were around them. They were on I-90. Snoqualmie Pass. "Elevation 3,022 feet" read the sign. He liked Mr. Diggs. But he didn't want to talk. The more he said, the more he would be remembered. And he didn't want to be remembered. He wanted to be invisible.

"That is one big bruise you've got, Travis the traveler."

Travis lifted his hand to his forehead. His father's elbow had struck him there last night. He didn't know it had left a mark. It felt sore and hot. He hadn't noticed it before. He'd only been thinking about getting away.

"Here."

Lawrence Diggs was holding out something. It was a tube of ointment.

"This will cover that up. Help it heal faster, son. I'm guessing you don't want to draw any attention. Right? When I saw you get on, I noticed you were traveling light."

Travis put some of the ointment onto his forehead. It made it feel cooler. He handed the tube back.

"Thank you, sir."

Lawrence Diggs nodded. "You're welcome. You have good manners, son. But don't bother calling me 'sir.' Just Diggs will do. That is what I answer to."

"Thank you . . . Diggs."

Diggs smiled. "You're welcome, Travis."

He crossed his arms and leaned back. Travis waited for him to ask questions. How did you get that bruise on your forehead? Who did that to you?

But Diggs didn't ask those things the way most adults did. The way his teachers did when he came to school with a black eye or a bloody lip. Travis always lied when they asked him those things. He'd say, "I fell down the stairs" or "I ran into a door."

Diggs just sat there. His silence was a peaceful sort of silence. It made Travis feel better.

"I'm going east to see my grandparents," Travis said.

"Hmm," Diggs replied. "Grandparents. That's good. Bet you'll be glad to see them."

Travis started talking. He talked about his grandparents. He told Diggs stories about them and where they lived. Diggs just listened, nodding now and then. Travis kept talking. He was surprised at how much he kept talking. When he finally stopped, the sun was high in the sky. More than an hour had passed. His throat felt dry.

Diggs reached down to a bag by his feet. He pulled out two cans of soda. He popped both open and passed one to Travis.

It was warm, but it tasted great. He hadn't thought about bringing anything to drink with him. All that he'd thought about was running away.

"Hungry?"

Diggs was handing him a sandwich from that same bag.

"You sure?" Travis asked.

"I always pack enough to share," Diggs chuckled. "Never know when I'll run into a hungry traveler."

Travis ate the sandwich. His stomach still hurt from being punched. But the sandwich tasted good. It was chicken with a peppery dressing.

"This is about the best sandwich I ever had," he said.

"Food eaten together always tastes better," Diggs said. "A man is supposed to share. That's what the old sacred books tell us. The Bible and the Koran both say that."

Travis nodded. He felt full and relaxed. He leaned back in his seat and yawned.

When he opened his eyes again, the bus was not moving. His face was pressed against the window. He could see a sign. "SPOKANE" it read.

He sat up. There was no one next to him. Diggs was gone. The whole bus was empty.

His backpack was on the seat where Mr. Diggs had been. It was open.

"Oh no!" Travis thought. "My money!"

He grabbed the pack and looked into it. The zipper pouch that held his cash was still there. He opened it. His money had not been touched. Then he noticed something else—a folded piece of paper.

"FOR TRAVIS THE TRAVELER" it read.

He unfolded it and a twenty-dollar bill fell out.

Travis picked it up. Then he saw that a poem had been written on the sheet of paper. The letters were carefully printed:

When a man is alone and on the road,
and he needs some help to share the load,
sometimes a stranger may give him a lift
and say, "Pass it on to return the gift."

Missoula

Travis had been on the road for two and a half days. He'd tried hitching, but no one stopped. After four hours he gave up. He went to the bus station and bought another ticket. It had taken him to Missoula. Missoula was a city in the state of Montana.

It was late afternoon. Travis walked from the bus station through the town, uncertain what to do. He was hungry, but he had to make his

money last. He might need it for an emergency.
Then he remembered Will's advice about food.
He waited until late evening and then went to
the alley behind a steakhouse after it closed. He
slowly opened the green lid of the dumpster. It
didn't make much noise. That was good. Make
too much noise and someone might hear. Then
they might come and chase you away.

Travis waited. He didn't hear anyone coming.

"Look first before you dive," Will had said.

Travis peered into the dumpster. There was
a streetlight shining into the alley. He could see
inside pretty well. There were cardboard boxes
in the bottom of the dumpster. It looked clean.
It didn't smell bad, like old, rotten food.

"You don't want one of those dirty dumpsters,"
Will had advised.

Travis waited, listening. Nothing was making
any sounds in the dumpster. That meant there
were probably no rats or raccoons or anything
that might bite him.

Travis levered himself up. He reached out and
grabbed the clear plastic bag on top. He could see
the food inside it. It looked good. Even through
the bag he could smell it. His mouth watered. He
hadn't eaten in more than twenty-four hours.

He took the bag to a doorway behind the
dumpster. There was light there from a streetlamp.

He tried to untie the bag. It was knotted too tight. He took out his lock-blade knife and cut the bag open.

Half a baked potato was the first thing he saw. He picked it up.

He was about to bite into it. Then he remembered something Grandma Kailin said.

Always give thanks, *nosis*.

"Nosis" meant "grandchild" in their language.

Travis nodded. He was so hungry. But giving thanks was more important.

He held the potato up to the light.

"Creator," he said, "I thank you for this good food."

Then he bit into it. He'd never tasted a better potato. He moved a paper napkin aside. There was a steak bone under the napkin. It still had meat stuck to the bone. There was other food too. Beans, baked carrots, pieces of chicken. There was even a half-full bottle of mineral water to drink.

After he ate, Travis felt happy. He was happier than he had been in a long time.

"I can do this," he said to himself. "I can."

He began to walk. He wasn't sure where he should go. He knew he had to get out of sight. He didn't want to attract attention from the police. They might stop him and ask him what he was doing. Then what would he do? He wasn't good at lying.

A woman pushing a shopping cart was just ahead of him. She hadn't been shopping. Not unless you could go shopping for junk of all kinds—things that looked like they were picked up from the street. Cans, bottles, tattered magazines, pieces of clothing. He noticed how dark her skin was. It was the skin of someone who lived outdoors. Maybe she was Indian too.

Travis walked up to her.

"Grandmother," he said. "Hello." He said it with respect in his voice. It was the way he had been taught to speak to older people.

She turned to look at him. She didn't look surprised or frightened that he spoke to her. Maybe it was the way he said it.

"Well," she said, "well, well, well." Then she smiled. It was a smile with no teeth. But it was a friendly smile.

"Grandmother," Travis said. "I don't know where to go."

The old woman nodded. "Home?" she said.

Travis shook his head. "No home."

"Ah. Ah, ah, ah," she said. She lifted her right hand and pulled back her sweater from her wrist. She looked at her wrist as if looking at a watch. There was no watch there. Then she looked back at Travis.

"Shelter?" she said.

Travis shook his head again. If anyone was looking for him, they might look at a shelter. He was not going to go to a shelter.

"Outdoors?" he asked.

The old woman nodded. She reached into her cart. She pulled out an old newspaper. She looked at it. Then she handed it to Travis.

"Map," she said. "Follow it."

Travis looked at the thick Sunday newspaper. It was two weeks old. It was not a map.

"Thank you, Grandmother," he said.

She said something back to him. He could not understand it. Maybe it was in another language, maybe a Native language like Cheyenne. As she spoke that language, her words were clearer. Her eyes were brighter. Then she pointed with her chin to her right.

"There," she said. "River. You go there."

He started to go. She grabbed his arm.

"Watch out for the twins," she said.

"Who are the twins?"

The old woman didn't answer. She just turned and shuffled away, pushing her cart.

When Travis got to the river, he saw she was right. There were places to find shelter. But it took a while to find a good spot.

The first place he tried was in a thick stand of little trees. A well-worn path led in, and Travis quietly followed it. Someone else was already there: a lanky man wearing blue jeans and a gray sweatshirt was curled up inside a piece of yellow foam rubber. He was snoring. Travis backed out without waking him.

The second place looked promising. It was under a cottonwood tree where the riverbank dropped down. Travis ducked his head under the exposed roots. The smell of urine was so strong that he backed out right away.

It was dark when he found the third spot near a footbridge that arched over the stream. He walked off the path and down the bank to look at it and the way the rocks and the bridge came together to make a sort of cave where someone could crawl in. He shone his penlight into it. It was a perfect shelter. He was surprised no one else was using it.

He thought about making a fire. There was a pile of old newspapers and dry brush nearby. The ground was blackened in one place back from the mouth of the cave. There was a faint smell of old smoke in the air, as well as something else. Maybe gasoline or lighter fluid. People who didn't know the right way to make fires would use those. Travis never did. His grandfather had told him that was a lazy way to do it and it showed no respect for the fire.

There was a half-moon in the sky and the penlight in his bag would give him enough additional light to find plenty of firewood. But then it was as if he heard his grandfather's voice speaking inside his head.

"Be careful," it said.

Something felt wrong. Maybe this place was too perfect. He piled some of the brush together at the back of the cave and then covered the brush with some of the newspaper so it looked like a person sleeping. Then he backed out of the cave.

He looked along the stream. There was a tangle of brush and bushes a few yards farther down the bank about sixty or seventy feet from the cave. Travis made his way down to the spot. It looked as if there was some open space under the low branches that he could crawl into. If it rained, he'd get wet. But this was Montana, not Seattle. The sky looked clear and the air felt dry. He got down on his belly. Pushing his pack ahead of him, he pulled the hood of his sweatshirt up over his head and wormed his way in. Small branches and thorns caught on his shoulders as he made his way forward, but he kept going. He went past a place where the branches opened up overhead and the moon shone down on him. He didn't stop there. He kept going. Deeper in would be safer.

Sure enough, when he got to the base of the largest bush, there was a space he could turn around in. The branches were like an umbrella over his head. The space was long enough for him to stretch out. He smoothed the dry earth with his palms, moving aside several round, baseball-sized stones. He spread part of the newspaper on the ground. He took the bag with the space blanket out of his pack. The bag was only the size of his hand, but when the thin blanket in it was unfolded, it covered his whole body.

Travis put the pack under his head and closed his eyes.

The sound of a vehicle approaching and then stopping on the nearby road woke him up. He heard the sound of the doors opening, feet crunching down on the gravel.

"Quiet," a voice whispered above him. "If somebody's in there, you'll wake 'em up."

"Hunh," a harsh second voice whispered back. "What you worried about, Chiv? Those drunk Indians don't never wake up."

"Not till it's too late, they don't."

Travis heard another sound, like a glass bottle tapped against metal. And the faint smell of gasoline wafted down to him. The hair on the back of his neck stood up.

"The twins," he thought. "That's who I'm hearing."

"Watch it, Walt. Don't spill that on me."

"Need some light."

A flashlight flicked on. Even though it was cupped by the hands of the person holding it—Walt, most likely—Travis could see the outline of two men standing at the back of a pickup truck. They were less than fifty feet from him on the road slightly above him.

"You hear something?" the man to the right whispered.

"Where?" The beam of the flashlight began sweeping in his direction. Travis lowered his head and closed his eyes. A person with closed eyes is harder to see. That was what Grampa Tomah said. He held his breath and began to count.

One, two, three . . .

"Hell, Chiv, there's nobody there. Just your imagination."

Travis opened his eyes again. The two men were moving onto the path that led under the bridge to the little cave where he'd been before.

"I was so right to feel wrong about that place," he thought.

He reached down and found two of the baseball-sized stones and then a third one that was slightly larger. He stood up slowly. He could

see the twins with their flashlight. They were
under the bridge at the mouth of the cave. One
of them lifted up something that glinted in the
light. A bottle filled with gasoline.

"Looks like there's one in there."

"Light it up, Chiv."

Fire flared up from Chiv's hand as he flicked
on a lighter.

That was when Travis whipped his arm back
and threw the first stone. His only aim was to
hit near them, but he did better than that.

"YEOW!" Chiv yelled as the stone hit his arm
and knocked the lighter from his grasp. Travis
threw the second stone, and somehow his aim
was even better. It hit the bottle of gasoline in
Walt's hand and shattered it, soaking the two
men with gasoline. If the lighter had not gone
out when it landed, they would have been set
on fire.

"OH MY GOD!" Walt yelled. "They're after
us. Run for it!"

The two men scrambled up the trail to their
truck and roared away, the wheels spraying
gravel.

A Good Ride

The sun woke Travis up early. There were a few bumps on his face from mosquito bites, but he had slept well. He felt rested and strong. He washed his face in the river and then went to the third place he'd considered as a shelter: the cave near the footbridge. The newspaper he'd been given had come in handy there.

He put his pack on his back and took a deep breath. Maybe Walt and Chiv would come back during the daylight. They hadn't seen him, but the sooner he got out of the area the better. He began running. Half an hour later he stopped. He felt he was far enough out of town, so he started hitching. He stood by the entrance to I-90 holding up his sign. He had made it on a thick piece of cardboard he found near the river, using a piece of charcoal to write. The charcoal was from a cold campfire someone had made near the riverbank.

"EAST?" was what he had written in big black letters. He also had drawn a smiley face on it. Travis had gotten the idea from Will Chan.

"When you're hitching," Will had said, "look friendly."

"A smiley face looks friendly," Travis thought.

"Brother Hawk," Will had told him, "the best rides are big rigs. If you get one of them to stop for you, you're in luck. They might take you five hundred miles."

No big rig stopped for him. The first ten he saw blew by him. They were picking up speed as they headed toward the bigger highway.

"I'm too close to the four-lane," Travis thought.

He moved back fifty yards, to be closer to the smaller road.

He set his feet and held up his sign.

He heard the gears shift as a blue semi turned and came his way. It wasn't going to stop. It came so close that Travis had to step back. The truck's huge tires kicked up so much dust it blinded him. His right foot sank into the rough, loose gravel. He stumbled and fell to one knee. He had to put his hand down to keep from rolling down the slope.

"Are you okay, partner?"

Travis looked up. Another truck had stopped. It wasn't a tractor trailer. This was a big silver Chevrolet pickup. A horse trailer was hooked to it. Words were written on the passenger-side door. He couldn't make them out at first, so he wiped the dust from his eyes and then read "COWBOY BOB, THE CALF-ROPING CHAMP."

"You okay?" the man in the truck said again. His face was hidden under a big hat, but his voice was friendly.

"I'm—" Travis started to say. Then he had to cough. There was dust in his mouth and in his nose too.

The man leaned over and opened the passenger-side door.

"Come on, partner. Get in."

Travis picked up his sign. He brushed the dust off his shirt and jeans. He swung his pack off his back and climbed up into the cab.

He could see the man's broad face now. It was as brown as an Indian face, but his eyes were blue. The man's hair was straw colored. His nose looked as if it had been broken more than once. A scar shaped like a lightning bolt ran down his right cheek.

The man grinned and touched the scar.

"Good one, huh? That was back from my bull-riding days. Big ol' Brahma named Satan hooked me there after I beat the buzzer."

The man held out his hand. Travis took it. The man didn't squeeze hard, but his hand was as rough as a cedar branch.

"Cowboy Bob's the name. And the rodeo's my road."

Travis nodded. "Thanks for stopping, sir. My name's Travis."

"Travis. Same as the name of one of my favorite singers. Makes it easy to remember. That's a little trick of mine when I meet someone. Tie their name to somebody famous. Travis."

Bob shifted the truck into gear and eased out onto the road. "So Travis, you're going east. Right? Don't be surprised I know that." He nodded at the sign. "I am awful good at picking up clues."

Travis smiled. "Thanks again, sir."

"Not 'sir.' Call me Bob or Cowboy Bob. Okay?

"Okay."

Bob settled back in his seat. He put one arm out the window. "Got me a long ride. Passing through the five B's: Butte, Belgrade, Bozeman, Billings, and Buffalo, Wyoming. Then on to Gillette. Gillette is where my sister Dolly lives. Same name as Dolly Parton. I plan to roost there till the next rodeo. Having someone along to talk to will help keep me awake. So you are doing me a favor, Travis. Just listen. Say 'Yup' every now and then. We got a deal?"

"Yes, sir. I mean yes, Bob."

Bob began to talk. He talked about being a rodeo person. He told Travis how he started when he was only twelve years old. He listed every bone in his body that had been broken. Seventeen altogether. He described every horse he'd owned. Ten of them.

"Old Jet Blue in the back there, he's the best of them all. Twelve years old and smart enough to teach fourth grade."

Travis did as Bob asked. He said "yes" or "yup" whenever Bob paused for breath. He enjoyed

Bob's stories. He thought he might like a life like
Cowboy Bob's. Maybe not as a cowboy, but a life
where he could travel on his own and do what
he wanted. That might be better than joining the
Marines. The hours sped by. They stopped twice.
The first was just past Bozeman to get gas and use
the restroom, and the second was at a roadside
diner. Travis tried to pay for his meal, but Bob
picked up the check.

"You're doing a fine job keeping me awake,
Travis. Consider it your wages."

Back in the truck, Bob turned on the radio.
"Hey," he said. "Listen to this song. It's a friend
of mine by the name of Wayne Earl Jones!"

> You don't need to take a Greyhound bus,
> you just need to take a chance on us.
> Baby, it's all right,
> Hold on, hold on tight.
>
> Don't need no ticket down to San Antone,
> you just need to have me for your own.
> Honey, it's all right,
> Hold on, hold on tight.
>
> Some say the road's the way to travel.
> Some say you need to get away.
> But I'll tell you, darling, on the level,
> that my love can take you all the way, hey!

You don't need to hitch along the I-90.
You just need to hook on up with me.
Baby, we got all night,
So hold on, hold on tight

Bob sang along with the song. When the song ended, Bob switched off the radio.

"I'd like to just keep that in my mind for a while. Know what I mean?"

Travis nodded. The song had been pretty good. But Bob's voice had been really bad. He was glad when Bob started talking again.

It got dark, but Bob kept going. The stars were bright and there was no moon.

"We are passing now through the Crow Indian Reservation," Bob said. "You're Indian, right? Are your people from out here?"

Travis hesitated. He didn't like to talk about being Indian. He knew how some people felt about Indians. He looked over at Bob. Bob had been friendly. Travis took a deep breath.

"No. My family is Passamaquoddy. They're from Maine."

Bob nodded. "Heard about them. Always been interested in other Indians. Believe it or not, I got relatives here. My mother's side is pure Absaroke. Bird people. Crow is just a name that got tacked on 'em."

Bob was silent for a while as they drove. They passed through a town called Garryowen. Then he pulled the truck over. There were no other vehicles on the road. Bob turned off the headlights and climbed out. He tilted his head back and stared up at the sky.

"Will you look at that?"

Travis stepped out. The gravel crunched under his feet. He lifted his chin. The heavens were filled with what looked like rivers of light. They streamed across the wide sky. They looked like waterfalls and fountains.

"The northern lights," Cowboy Bob said. His voice was filled with wonder.

Travis felt a lump in his throat. "I never saw them before," he said.

"And now you will never forget them, little brother."

They stood there for a while.

"Well," Bob said, "guess we better get going."

"Yup," Travis said. "Thank you."

"Nope," Bob replied. "Thank those dancers in the sky."

They continued driving. Bob was talking less now. But he did point a few things out. "Little Bighorn Battlefield is over there," he said. "That is where those Lakotas and Cheyennes wiped out George Armstrong Custer." Bob chuckled. "But us Crows were on the wrong side that day. One of my great-grampas was scouting for old Yellow Hair."

Travis didn't remember falling asleep. When he opened his eyes, the truck was stopped. He was alone in the truck. Then the door next to him opened. A dark-haired woman was standing there.

"My name's Dolly," she said. "Same as that country singer."

"I'm Travis."

"So," Dolly said, "come on, Travis."

She took his pack in one hand and his sign in the other. Travis followed her into the house. Dolly dropped the pack by a red leather couch. There was a clock on the wall above the couch. It was five a.m.

"Bob's already in bed and snoring. That means the spare room is taken. Will this do?"

A pillow and blanket were on the couch.

Travis nodded. It was hard to keep his eyes open. "Thank you, ma'am."

"Dolly," she said. "Same as the singer. The bathroom's there. Use the green towel. Good night now."

"Good night, Dolly."

Ten minutes later Travis was curled up on the couch. It was a little small, but it was better than the ground.

"There really are good people in the world," he thought. Then he fell asleep.

Good People

olly made breakfast for them the next morning. There were eggs, thick pieces of ham, and homemade bread that was still warm. There was honey and raspberry jam. Travis hadn't had a breakfast like this for a long time.

"Good," he said between mouthfuls. "Really good."

"Nice to have someone who appreciates my cooking," Dolly said. "Not like some people." She punched Bob in the arm, but not hard.

"Ow!" Bob said, kidding. "That's my roping arm. I think you broke it."

"Grow up, little brother," Dolly replied. Travis liked the way she said that. There was warmth and teasing in her voice. He could tell she really loved her brother.

Bob held up his cup. "The least you can do is give me some more coffee for my pain."

"Ha!" Dolly said. But she poured more coffee for him anyway.

Bob took a sip.

"Good coffee," he said. "But it's not cowboy coffee."

"What's cowboy coffee?" Travis asked.

Bob smiled. "It's strong." Then he waited.

Travis understood what he was supposed to say. "How strong is it?"

"It's so strong," Bob replied, "that when you put a spoon in it, the spoon dissolves."

They all laughed. It felt warm in Dolly's little house. Travis wished he could stay. But he knew that wasn't possible. He looked at Dolly.

"Thank you, ma'am," he said. "I mean, Dolly."

Dolly nodded. "I guess you'll be going now? Bob told me you need to get to your grandma and grandpa's."

"That's right," Travis said. Then Dolly looked out back. "Could you do a little job for me before you go?"

"I'd be glad to."

"Those bushes need trimming. I'll pay you to do it."

Travis shook his head. "This breakfast is pay enough."

"Nope," Dolly said. "Trim them good and I'll pay you $20. Then Bob will drive you out to where you can hitch a ride. Deal?"

"Deal," Travis said.

Bob pulled a pair of gloves off a shelf and handed them to Travis. "Watch out for thorns."

Travis worked on the bushes for two hours. Some were roses. Some were cedars. He did a good job. He took out dead branches and shaped the bushes. He had trimmed shrubs before. It was one of the things he'd learned to do to make money—money that his father usually took from him to buy alcohol.

Dolly came out to see what he had done.

"My Lord!" she said. "That is as good as a professional gardener would do." She handed Travis two bills. One was a twenty. One was a ten. Thirty dollars, not twenty.

"That's too much," Travis said.

"No," Dolly replied. "You earned every cent."

"I appreciate it, Dolly," Travis said.

"Bob is ready to take you to the road," Dolly said. "Our people don't say goodbye the way most white folks do. Have a good road. That's what we say."

She took Travis by the hand. "Anytime you come through here, you stop in. Right?"

"Right," Travis said. He would have said more, but it was hard to talk. Something was caught in his throat. Three times now people had been so nice to him. First Diggs, and then the old woman who might have been Cheyenne. And now Bob and Dolly. But he had to leave them behind.

"If I can ever do anything to help others," Travis thought, "I am going to do it."

Bob dropped him at a place where two roads came together.

"This is a good spot," Bob said. "Most folks pause for that stop sign. Now and then, some even stop. Good luck, partner. Have a good road."

Bob was right. Travis stood there for only ten minutes before an old, beat-up Ford truck stopped.

There were four people in the cab. They were all brown-skinned and had mustaches. They looked like brothers. The one closest to the window on the passenger side leaned his head out.

"Only going as far as Spearfish," the man said. He looked as if he was about thirty years old. "Just fifty miles. And you have to ride in the back. That okay?"

"Sure," Travis replied. "Anything will help."

"Cool. You can sit in our grandma's chair. We just got it fixed and we're bringing it to her."

Travis climbed in the back, where there was a big green reclining chair. It was tied down with ropes. He sat in it, facing backward.

The gears ground as the truck lurched forward. It felt as if it might fall apart. But as soon as the truck picked up enough speed, it ran smoothly. Still, it wasn't fast. Every other car on the road passed them. Some honked their horns and looked annoyed. Some smiled and waved at Travis. He smiled and waved back at them. The sun was shining. The wind was whipping his hair around his face.

"This is a good road," he thought.

Someone tapped his shoulder. A hand had reached around the chair. It was another one of the four men. He had slid open the back window.

"Want some?" the man said. He held out a donut.

Travis took it. It was covered with sugar that stuck to his fingers. "Thanks," Travis said.

The man nodded and slid the window shut again.

Travis broke off a small piece of the donut. He held it up to the sun. "Thank you," he said. Then he tossed a little piece of donut onto the roadside. It was something his grandparents had taught him to do, a way to share what you were given with nature.

They passed through Moorcraft and went another ten or fifteen miles. Then they pulled over to the side of the road.

"Break time," the driver said. He nodded toward some nearby trees. "Bathroom's over there."

Travis understood. There wasn't really a bathroom. But you could relieve yourself behind those trees. Two of the brothers were already over there doing that.

When Travis got back to the truck, all four men were just standing there. They were facing north. One of them beckoned to Travis.

"Up there, son. Look up there."

Travis looked. He wasn't sure what he should look for.

"*Tsoai-talee*," the man said. He looked to be the oldest brother.

"They call it Devil's Tower," the youngest brother said. "Remember that movie? *Close Encounters*?"

Travis nodded. He'd seen it on the Syfy channel at Lenny and Lenore's house.

"It's a sacred place for our people," the oldest brother said. "It rose up from the ground to save some children from a bear trying to get them. You can see its claw marks on the side. Then those children stepped up into the sky and became stars. Think of that."

They stood there for a while, all of them thinking of that.

"Okay," the oldest brother said.

They piled into the truck. Travis climbed in the back. The gears ground again. The truck lurched and shook even worse than before as they pulled back onto the road.

They didn't stop in Spearfish but instead drove through the town before stopping.

"Okay," the oldest brother said. "It's a good spot here to grab a ride."

Travis hopped down. The truck turned around and headed back into Spearfish. None of the brothers looked back as they drove away.

"I never learned their names," Travis thought. "But that's okay."

He added them to his mental list of good people.

Sioux Falls

Travis looked down the road. He had been standing there for hours and no one had stopped. It was dark. He was near a town called White Lake in South Dakota. It had taken him two more rides to get here from Sturgis.

A big car was heading his way. It looked like a Cadillac. Travis held up his sign. The car shot past him close, so close the sign was almost knocked from his hand. Then he saw the red flash of brake lights, bright as fire in the dark. The car screeched to a stop fifty yards beyond him.

An arm reached out the driver's window and waved to him. It looked like a woman's arm. Charm bracelets dangled from her wrist.

"Come on," a woman's voice shouted. "Come on! I haven't got all day."

Travis ran up to the car. He opened the door.

"Get on in."

He had barely gotten into the seat when the woman thrust her foot down on the accelerator. The wheels spun on the gravel and then squealed as they caught the pavement. Travis almost fell out. He grabbed the door handle and pulled the door shut. The car was still picking up speed. He clicked his seat belt. There was a familiar smell in the car. Too familiar. It smelled like his father's breath when he'd been drinking.

"Oh no," Travis thought.

He looked over at the woman. It was hard to tell how old she was. She was wearing a yellow pantsuit. She had long auburn hair and a lot of makeup on her face. She smiled at him. Her smile was crooked.

"What a nice-looking boy," she said. Then she pushed her foot down even harder on the gas.

Travis tried not to look her way. She was waving her arm at him as she talked. He was glad it was a big car and her arm couldn't reach him.

"You can come to my house, honey," she told him. "Just over the border in Iowa. You're a nice boy, aren't you?"

The miles flashed by.

"What can I do?" Travis thought. "What can I do?"

It was after midnight when they drove into Sioux Falls. There was a stoplight. As soon as the car stopped, Travis opened his door. He jumped out.

"Where you going?" the woman said. Her voice was slurred. "We're not there yet."

"Thank you, ma'am," Travis said. "This is far enough."

"You come back," the woman yelled. She held up a cell phone. "Come back now or I'll call the cops!"

Travis ran. It was the only thing he could think to do. He could hear the woman screaming from her car. One block, two blocks, three blocks. Finally he couldn't hear her anymore.

Maybe she's given up. Maybe she'll just keep going.

He kept running. The streets were empty. He was the only one around.

"I'll be okay," he thought. "I'll be okay."

He ran down a hill toward a huge brick building that looked old. Maybe it was some sort of hotel. He turned the corner and almost ran into a black-and-white car parked facing the other way. A red light was on top of that car. A police car! With a policeman standing next to it. He was talking into a microphone clipped to his shoulder.

Travis stopped and looked at the policeman. The policeman looked at him.

"No," Travis thought. "No!" He turned and began to run again.

"Stop!" the policeman yelled.

Travis ran harder. There were big statues all along the street. If he wasn't being chased he would have stopped to look at them. One was a huge stone walrus with its baby. Another was an eagle made out of scrap iron. He turned a corner and leaped over a bunch of garbage bags piled on the sidewalk under a streetlight. He could hear the policeman's feet slapping the pavement behind him. But the sound of the man's feet was getting further away. Travis was faster than most boys his age and faster than most men. He ran easily. His heart was pounding, but he wasn't

running out of breath. He really did have the gift
of running.

He was getting away.

He grabbed a drainpipe on the side of a red
brick building and used it to spin himself into
a narrow alleyway. That was a mistake. There
was something in front of him. It was fifty feet
ahead, visible in the pool of light from a window.
It was a mother cat lying on her side, right in the
middle of the narrow passage. There were seven
little kittens feeding from her.

"I could leap over them," Travis thought.

But would the policeman behind him do
that? Would he step on one of those kittens as
he chased Travis?

Travis could not bear the thought of that.
If one of those kittens got hurt it would be his
fault. He stopped. The mother cat looked up at
him but didn't look worried.

"Move," Travis said. The cat didn't move.

Travis knelt down. He picked up a handful
of kittens and gently placed them to the side
behind a box. They would be safe there. He
picked up a second handful. The mother cat was
standing now. She was stretching and looking
lazy.

A hand grasped Travis by the shoulder. He
looked up and saw the policeman. He was tall

and skinny. There was sweat on his face. He was
breathing hard.

"What are you, boy, some kind of track star?"
he said, panting.

Travis didn't answer. "I'm an idiot," he thought.
But he didn't say that out loud. He just kept
quiet.

The policeman bent down. "Don't you know
there's a curfew here for teenagers?"

Travis could answer that. "No, sir," he said. "I
was just passing through. Someone just dropped
me off here. I'd hitched a ride."

Travis waited. Had the drunk woman called
the police?

"Why'd you run?"

"I don't know, sir. I just got scared, I guess."

The man studied Travis's face in the light from
the window. Travis could see the policeman's face
in that light too. He had thick brown hair under
his cap. Travis noticed the man needed a shave.
The man's brow was knitted. His lips were tight.
His face was red from running. He looked angry.
His name was written on a strip of metal pinned
to his shirt: "Sergeant Ray Abourezk."

"I am going to jail," Travis thought.

"Stand up," Sergeant Abourezk said. His voice
wasn't angry. It was businesslike. A policeman
doing his job.

Travis stood.

"Lean against the wall."

Travis leaned. The sergeant took the backpack off Travis's shoulders. He ran his hands down Travis's body.

"No weapons?"

"Just my belt knife, sir," Travis said. "But it's not a weapon. It's a tool."

The sergeant took the knife off Travis's belt.

"Now he's going to handcuff me," Travis thought. But the sergeant didn't do that.

"Turn around," he said.

Travis turned.

The sergeant lifted his hand to his chin and looked at Travis.

"Got any ID?"

Travis pointed at his backpack with his chin. "In there, sir."

"Will you show me what's in there?"

"Yes, sir."

The sergeant stepped back a little. "Open it and dump everything on the ground."

Travis bent down and undid the straps. He carefully emptied the contents onto the pavement.

The sergeant pointed at the deerskin bag. "What's that?"

"A fire-making kit."

"Open it."

Travis opened the bag. He carefully took out the contents, naming them as he did. "Flint and steel, tinder, nylon cord for a bow drill, steel wool, a battery." He looked up at the sergeant, who was shaking his head.

"Fire-making," the sergeant said. "Okay, put it away. Now hand me the wallet."

Travis did that. The sergeant opened it and looked at the ID. He looked at Travis. He looked at the ID again.

"Travis Hawk," the policeman read aloud. "Washington State driver's license?"

"Yes, sir. I just got it. I took Driver's Education. I got an A in it. I don't have a car. But I do have a license now."

"I'm talking too much," Travis thought. He suddenly remembered something that Will Chan had told him. When a policeman stops you, keep your answers simple. Police like to get you to start talking. The more you say, the worse it gets for you.

Travis shut his mouth.

"Where you going, Travis Hawk?"

"What can I say?" Travis thought. Then he remembered what Grandma Kailin often said. Tell the truth. That's easier to remember than a lie.

"Maine, sir."

"All that way and this," the sergeant gestured at the few items in Travis's pack, "is all you have with you?"

"Yes, sir. Do you know who John Muir was?"

"No. Who was he?"

"Why did I say that? I'm talking too much again," Travis thought. But now he had to answer.

"My grandpa told me about John Muir. He wrote about nature. He walked all the way across the country. All he took with him was an extra pair of socks, a knife, a notebook, and a pencil."

The sergeant shook his head again. "So why are you going to Maine?"

"I'm going to my grandparents', sir. They live there."

"What about your parents?"

"My mother, she . . . passed on. My Dad is out of work. So it would be easier for me to live with my grandma and grandpa in Maine."

Sergeant Abourezk raised one eyebrow. "Maine? How are you getting there?"

"First by bus. But mostly hitching, sir. I don't have a lot of money. I'm doing okay, though. I started three days ago in Seattle, and I got this far."

The sergeant whistled softly. "From Seattle to. Sioux Falls? A thousand miles all on your own?" He shook his head.

"People have been really nice, sir," Travis said.

Sergeant Abourezk smiled for the first time. "And you're a nice kid, aren't you?" He nodded. "Yup! I saw what you did with this mother cat and her kittens. If you hadn't done that, you would have likely gotten away."

"Yes, sir, I would."

The sergeant laughed. "Travis, no one in the last ten years has called me sir as often as you have. I don't hear that word much on this job. Let me ask you another question or two. You tell me the truth, okay?"

"Yes, sir."

"Okay. Question one: You break any laws?"

Travis shook his head. "Not any I know about, sir."

Sergeant Abourezk laughed again. "First you run like a track star. Then you answer like a lawyer. Let me put it another way. You got a guilty conscience about anything?"

Travis thought about that. He'd left his father without telling him. But he didn't feel guilty about that. He also didn't feel guilty about putting that bag of stuff in Mannie's room. And he certainly didn't feel guilty about jumping out of the drunk woman's car.

"No, sir. Not at all."

"Have you taken anything that wasn't yours?"

Travis started to shake his head. Then he stopped. "Well, I did take some food out of a dumpster. But it had been thrown away, and it was still good, and . . ."

Travis stopped talking. He was saying too much again. Why was he doing that? And he was really tired. He hadn't realized how tired he was. The mother cat came and rubbed against his leg. He looked down at her. So did the policeman.

Sergeant Abourezk patted him on the shoulder. "Okay, Travis. Enough questions." He knelt down and petted the mother cat. "Now help me with these guys."

Travis lifted up the mother cat and two of the kittens. The sergeant picked up the other ones. He pulled a cardboard box from the trash.

"This will do for now," he said.

They put the eight cats in the box. Travis lifted the box and looked down at them. The mother rolled onto her side and the kittens started nursing. She began to purr.

"My cruiser's four blocks that way. Follow me."

"Am I under arrest?"

The sergeant looked back at him. "No, son. We're going to the shelter."

"Oh no," Travis thought. "Another homeless shelter? What if they've heard about me running away? I'll get sent back to Seattle."

He thought again about running. But he couldn't do that carrying the mother cat and her kittens. Plus the policeman had his backpack and his knife. He needed them. He followed the sergeant to his police car.

The sergeant opened the back door. "Watch your head."

Travis put the box with the cats in it on the seat. Then he climbed in. The sergeant shut the door behind him.

Travis had never been in a police car before. There was a mesh screen between him and the front seat. He could see a small computer on the dashboard. A shotgun was holstered on the driver's-side door. There were papers and a clipboard on the front seat.

The sergeant slid in behind the wheel. He spoke into a microphone. Travis couldn't understand most of what he said. Then he put down the mic and dialed a number on his phone. Once again he had a conversation, most of which Travis couldn't hear . . . until the last few words.

"You're sure about that? Yup? Okay, Auntie!"

Sergeant Abourezk turned to him. "Buckle up."

Travis fastened his seat belt. The car slid out from the curb as the sergeant spun the wheel. Travis didn't remember closing his eyes, but when he opened them, the car had stopped again. The box with the cats was gone. He blinked and looked through the window. They were in front of a low white building. The sergeant was walking back toward the car. He unlocked the door and climbed in.

"Sorry to lock you in, son. Standard operating procedure. Didn't want you hijacking my vehicle while I was gone."

He laughed after saying that.

"Should I get out here?" Travis asked.

The sergeant looked back over his shoulder at him. "Why? You want to check in at the animal shelter with your new friends?" He laughed again.

Animal shelter? Not a homeless shelter?

"Where are we going now?"

"You'll see."

Travis watched out the window as they drove. They went over a bridge.

"Sioux Falls is down there," the sergeant said. He pointed out the window to his left. "Too dark to see much now. You can check them out tomorrow."

They pulled into a parking lot at a sort of shopping mall. Above the lot was an elevated line of stores and restaurants.

"Up there," the sergeant said. "Follow me."

They went up the steps, passing by dark storefronts. No one else was around.

The sergeant paused. "You're pretty strong, right? Good at carrying things?"

"I guess so," Travis said. "I don't mind working."

"Thought not."

They had stopped in front of a closed restaurant with a sign that read "Sanaa's Gourmet Mediterranean."

"Best Syrian food in town."

Travis got the joke. "The only Syrian food in town?"

Sergeant Abourezk laughed. "Yup! You got it, young man. But it's also the best food in town. Maybe the whole state."

He rapped on the door. A light came on from the back. Then a dark-haired woman came forward. She didn't look young, but there was a warm smile on her face.

"She must have been beautiful when she was young," Travis thought.

She opened the door.

"Hello, Aunt Sanaa," the sergeant said.

"Is this my young worker?" she asked.

"Yup."

She looked at Travis. "Can you move things? Heavy things?"

Travis nodded. "Yes, ma'am. At least I can try."

Sergeant Abourezk laughed. "See what I mean? He's an honest one."

"Polite, too," Aunt Sanaa said. "He'll do."

Travis looked at the sergeant. It was late and he was confused.

The sergeant smiled. "Okay, son. Here's the deal. You can help out for a few hours tomorrow cleaning out a storeroom. You'll be taking the place of someone who called in sick. In return you get a place to stay tonight, and you get fed tomorrow. Then my uncle Jim will give you a ride. He's on his way to LaCrosse, Wisconsin. Sound good?"

"Sounds wonderful," Travis said. "Thank you so much, Sergeant."

The sergeant took his hand. "Ray," he said. "You can call me Ray, Travis. We cat rescuers operate on a first-name basis."

Then he handed Travis back his knife and pack.

"Good luck getting to your grandparents'."

"Thank you, sir."

Sergeant Abourezk laughed. "What did you say?"

"Thank you, Ray."

The Senator

ravis woke up feeling confused. The bed underneath him was so much softer than the ground he'd been sleeping on that it made his back hurt. Where was he?

He looked around. He was in a small room lined with shelves of boxes and jars. Food.

He sat up. The flowered quilt that had been placed over him slid off. He put his feet on the floor. His sneakers were there. So was his backpack. He'd slept in his clothes.

Then he remembered. He was on a cot in the back room of the restaurant. The place Sergeant Ray had taken him last night.

He smelled something. Food was being cooked in the next room. It didn't smell like anything he'd ever eaten before, but it smelled really good.

"Are you awake now, little bird?" a voice called from another room. "You are the last bird to rise this morning."

It was a pleasant voice, a musical voice. Why did it sound familiar? Then he recognized who it belonged to. It was the voice of Aunt Sanaa, the woman who owned the restaurant. "There is a washroom back there, my young worker. Use it and then come and eat."

Travis went into the small washroom. He combed his hair back with his fingers. He breathed on the palm of his hand and smelled it. He hoped his breath wasn't too bad. There was no mouthwash. He rinsed his mouth with water and then walked out into the kitchen. The kitchen opened into the restaurant, which was not yet open for the day. But there was food on a small table.

Aunt Sanaa smiled at him. "You are hungry? Sit and eat. Then I shall work you until your fingers are worn to the bone."

Travis worked all through the morning. The storeroom needed to be cleaned and there were many things to move. It was hard work, but not too hard. When Travis was done, Aunt Sanaa came to inspect.

"Fine," she said. "And faster than I expected. Did you take any break?"

"I didn't really need a break, ma'am."

She looked him up and down, from his feet to his forehead. "My husband's nephew is a good judge of men, Travis. That is why he brought you here. You are a fine young man. Your parents must be proud of you."

Travis started to say something, but the words caught in his throat. He blinked because his eyes were burning. Aunt Sanaa did not notice. She had already turned away.

"Come," she said, gesturing back at him. "Bring your things. The car is outside."

It was more than just a car. It was a big black limousine. The back door opened as he approached. A balding older man with a friendly, intelligent smile leaned forward and gestured to him.

"Get in, get in."

As Travis leaned forward, the man grabbed his hand with surprising strength and pulled Travis in, swinging him over to sit next to him.

"Let's go," the man said, pulling the door shut. "Drive on, Milton!" The car shot forward, pushing Travis back into the seat as it accelerated.

The older man swung his hand to indicate where they were. "Not the way I usually travel. But when a limo gets sent to take you to a meeting, that limo gets used. That's one of the perks of having been a famous person. Or should I say infamous?"

The man laughed. It was a warm, friendly laugh that put Travis at ease. The man looked at Travis with shrewd eyes.

"I see quite a story in you, young man." He held out his hand. "James Abourezk," he said. "Just call me Jim. And you?"

Travis took his hand. This time the man grasped him gently. An Indian handshake, not one of those white man ones where your hands get squeezed and your fingers almost get broken.

"Travis, sir. Travis Hawk."

"Indian, right? Or 'Native American,' as our politically correct white folks say these days."

"Yes, sir."

"But not local. You don't have a Lakota look about you. One of the eastern nations?"

Travis just nodded this time. He wasn't sure what to say or if he even needed to say anything at all. The man was doing enough talking for the both of them.

Jim Abourezk laughed. "You're thinking that I'm monopolizing the conversation? Don't bother to answer that. I already hear it often enough from my wife. It's the result of a few years in Washington. Though not nearly few enough if you were to listen to my Republican colleagues."

"Yes, sir," Travis said.

That prompted an even larger laugh from the former senator. Then he kept talking. He was interesting to listen to, even if Travis knew little about politics. He talked about things Travis had only heard about in history class. About what President Nixon did, and about being a liberal senator from a non-liberal state and then losing his seat.

"To a clown. And a crooked one at that."

Travis closed his eyes. He hadn't realized how tired he was. When he opened them again, it was dark outside and the senator was no longer talking. He was leaning back and snoring. Travis shifted in his seat and the senator sat up and looked outside.

"Ah," he said, catching sight of a roadside sign. "Travis, have you been asleep?"

"Yes, sir."

The senator nodded. "Just as well. All you missed was most of the state of Wisconsin."

The sun was rising as they crossed the bridge over the Mississippi. The waters were turning shades of color Travis had never seen before.

The senator nodded. "Even at my age, seeing this still brings a lump to my throat. America the beautiful. It's a wonderful land we have, young man. Isn't it?"

"It is, sir," Travis said.

"And still, after the way your people have been treated—and the way my own Arab people are being treated now—we love it, don't we?"

"We do, sir. We really do."

"There's more good than bad here, you know."

Travis nodded. He knew that to be true. He knew it from what he'd experienced the past few days.

They were just passing a truck stop. Big tractor trailers were parked in front of it. The senator leaned forward and tapped on the window.

"Stop here, Milton. Thank you." he said.

The driver pulled the car over.

"Travis, it has been a pleasure traveling with you," the senator said. "Hope you didn't mind my talking your ear off. Those semis there are all long-haul vehicles, and I can't think of a better place for you to attempt to get a ride east."

He opened the door and Travis climbed out, his legs stiff from the long ride. The senator handed his backpack to him.

"There's an old saying in Arabic," the senator said, "to wish a traveler a good journey." He chuckled. "Unfortunately, I don't know it." He shook Travis's hand. "Good luck, young man. Keep loving this land—even if our politicians don't always deserve it."

"I will," Travis said. "Thank you, sir."

The door shut and the black limo drove away.

Big Rig

The sun was beating down hard on Travis's head. Drops of sweat were running down his cheeks like glistening beads. Huge semis were pulling out of the truck stop. Some of them were hauling two trailers. He heard the gears shift and the whoosh of the air brakes. One after another went by without pausing.

Travis kept holding up his sign with one hand while waving with the other. He smiled as best he could, even though he was beginning to feel like a wilted plant. Was anyone going to stop before he died of heat stroke?

Just as he had that thought, the next truck coming out of the driveway pulled over. It wasn't as large as any of the semis that had passed him. It made up for its size with its color, though. It was painted with rainbows, rain-forest trees, and tropical birds. The words "Miami Momma" were written on its side.

"Miami?" Travis thought. That was about as far south from Maine as you could get on the East Coast. Did he really want to accept a ride from a truck going that way? On the other hand, did he want to end up like an overcooked hamburger?

The truck had stopped fifty yards beyond him.

WHOONK! WHOONK!

The driver was blowing the tractor trailer's horn. It was a message for him to hurry up if he was coming. Travis began to run.

When he reached the truck, the door on the passenger side swung open as he grabbed the rail to climb up. It was so bright in the sunlight that he couldn't see the driver inside the cab. But then he heard a voice.

"Climb on in."

It was a woman's voice.

Travis hesitated. The last ride he'd accepted from a woman hadn't ended well.

"Come on," the woman said. "I'm on the clock and time's a wastin'."

Travis still couldn't see the woman, but her voice sounded friendly. It also had a Southern accent.

"Thank you, ma'am," he said. "But are you going east?"

The woman laughed. Her laugh was a deep one, and somehow it was reassuring.

"You read my name, eh? Don't let it fool you. Miami is just where I'm from and where I wish I could be. That's why Rufus painted our truck up this way. He knew it would tickle me to have a whole jungle on the side of a refrigerated rig. I'm taking this load of lettuce all the way to Bangor, Maine. That far enough east for you?"

Travis climbed in and shut the door. The door was so tight that his ears popped. The air in the truck was as cool as a late-autumn breeze, and it smelled almost as fresh. He looked at the woman. He could see her face now. It was red, as if she'd just scrubbed it. She had a big nose and a wide mouth, red hair, and eyes as blue as the sky. She wasn't young at all. Probably as old as forty.

She stuck out a hand. "Mimi," she said. "Mimi Kinnell. And you?"

"Travis. Travis Hawk, ma'am."

Mimi Kinnell grinned so wide that Travis could see she had teeth missing on either side of her mouth. "Hawk? The way you sprinted to my truck, you ought to be called Deer! You are one fast runner."

"I guess so," Travis said.

Mimi Kinnell turned her gaze toward her side mirror, worked the gears, and pushed down on the accelerator. The truck swung out smoothly onto the road and began to pick up speed.

"So where out east you heading?" she asked, her eyes flicking down on a small computer monitor.

"Maine," Travis said. "I am so glad you picked me up. I can't believe you're going there."

"Believe it," she said, tapping the monitor with her index finger. "Family there? In Maine, I mean."

"Yes, ma'am," Travis replied. "My grandparents."

"Nice. I've got me two grandkids. Don't see them enough. Driving this rig makes it hard for me to get back to see them. Been even harder without Rufus."

"Rufus," Travis thought. It was the second time she'd mentioned that name.

Mimi Kinnell turned toward Travis as if she had heard his thoughts. She nodded at him. "My husband," she said. "We always drove this route together."

Travis nodded. He thought he knew what she was going to say next, that her husband had died. But she didn't say it. Maybe she knew she didn't have to say it from the look in Travis's eyes.

Mimi Kinnell pointed over her shoulder at a backseat single bed. "We used to take turns sleeping on long hauls. You tired?"

"A little," Travis said.

"Good. Here's the drill. You sleep till it gets dark. Then you help keep me awake while I drive through the night. In return I give you the lift to Maine and buy you a few burgers along the way. We got a deal, partner?"

"Deal," Travis said.

"Good," Mimi Kinnell grinned. She pulled a pair of ear buds out of her pocket. Travis could hear the faint sounds of a country song coming from them. She inserted them into her ears. "Now I got me a date with my boy Merle Travis. You catch some shut-eye."

Travis lay back on the bed. He'd never slept in a truck before and the mattress was thin. But the small, hard pillow had a familiar scent. It took him a moment to recognize it as balsam. The pillow had been stuffed with balsam fir needles that smelled just like the trees around his grandparents' cabin. He closed his eyes, took a deep breath, and relaxed.

The next thing he knew, he felt the truck slowing down and turning. He sat up and leaned forward from the sleeping compartment. It was night and the bright lights of a big city with tall buildings were off to his right. They were so bright they almost didn't look real to him.

"You've been snoring away, partner," Mimi Kinnell said. "We are now in the windy city of Chicago."

Travis shook his head. This was the second time he had fallen asleep as hundreds of miles passed by. Maybe if he'd just slept long enough he could have woken up in Maine. But he also felt as if he'd slept too much. His lips were dry, and his tongue felt as if it was covered with fuzz. And he was groggy and felt a little dizzy.

Mimi Kinnell leaned over to look at him. "You look a little out of it, partner. When was the last time you ate?"

Travis thought about that. He wasn't sure. "Yesterday," he said, "I guess."

Mimi Kinnell snorted. "Huh! There's no way you're going to keep me awake if you're fainting from hunger. Come on, let's get you refueled."

Three hamburgers, two jumbo fries, and a milkshake later—plus a trip to the truck-stop bathroom—Travis found himself on the road again.

"You either talk or you listen good," Mimi Kinnell said, sipping from the huge coffee mug she'd filled at the stop.

Travis did his best to do both. He listened to her stories of crossing America again and again with Rufus by her side. "Childhood sweethearts, we was, and all we both ever wanted to do was travel. Just about a perfect life for us, wasn't it?"

Then Travis talked. He talked about the things his grandparents had told him, even telling her some of the old stories they had shared. He talked about the experiences he'd had so far on the road. But he said nothing about either his father or their life together before he ran away, and Mimi didn't ask. The miles of the I-90 and state after state sped by. They went through South Bend and Toledo and Cleveland and Erie and Buffalo without stopping or slowing down from the seventy miles per hour she averaged.

"Rufus called me his iron woman," Mimi said. "He never saw anyone who kept at it hour after hour like me. I never took no pills neither. It just takes coffee to keep me going." There was both pride and a little catch in her voice as she said that.

It was midmorning when she pulled into a New York State Thruway rest stop.

"We'll eat here, then you can take the cot again. Unless you've learned how to drive this rig by watching me."

Travis shook his head. "No, ma'am, I have not."

Mimi laughed and slapped the steering wheel affectionately. "I was just joking, partner. No way I'd ever give over the wheel of my rain-forest baby. But, hey, maybe you want to give your grandparents a call and let them know where you are?"

She pulled an iPhone out of her pocket, unplugged the ear buds, and held it out toward Travis.

He shook his head. "No, thank you. They don't have a phone . . . and I don't have one of those either."

Mimi shook her head. "What? No Twitter? No Facebook friends? Are you the only teenager in the world who doesn't use one of these?"

Travis grinned. "I didn't say that. May I?" He took the phone from Mimi, thought for a second, and quickly Googled his own name.

Nothing came up. No "endangered" or "missing" notice. Good!

Then he held the phone up to his mouth.

"Siri," he said, "what's the weather tomorrow for Bangor, Maine?"

"The weather forecast for Bangor, Maine, tomorrow is sunny with a high of seventy-five degrees," the calm female voice replied.

Travis handed the phone back. "I used to have a phone. But right now I just can't afford one. And I guess I don't really need it."

When they took to the highway again, Travis was back in the sleeping compartment. But he couldn't sleep. Too many thoughts were going through his mind. One of them was how he'd be greeted by his grandparents. He knew they loved him, but would they want him to be staying with them—even for the few months until he could enlist?

He turned his head so he could see the road signs. They passed the signs for Rochester, Syracuse, Utica, and then Albany. Hours were going by as he watched, neither sleeping nor fully awake. They left New York and joined the Mass Pike. After a brief rest stop, they were back on the road. The night closed in around them, with Travis sitting next to Mimi, talking and listening as before.

At one point, at a pause in their conversation, Travis looked at Mimi with amazement. It really was just as her late-husband Rufus had said. She was like a person made of iron. Never tiring, never losing focus as she drove. "If there was a road to the moon," Travis thought, "she could drive it."

Three hours later they passed Boston and headed northeast. Another rest stop, then they were passing through Portsmouth in the narrow part of southern New Hampshire.

"Only two hundred miles to Bangor from here, partner," Mimi said.

Another dawn was breaking when Travis stepped down out of the cab. He'd been on the road with Mimi for a whole day and a half. He breathed in the air. It was just as he remembered it, not the ocean smell from their drive along the coast. It was the scent of evergreens, of countless miles of pine trees. His grandparents' cabin was in the middle of a pine forest to the north of the road. Their ninety acres could only be reached by logging roads. The property was in the middle of what had been a hunting ground and home for their people for thousands of years.

"You look happy, partner."

Travis turned to look at Mimi. The grin on her face was so broad that with her reddish skin she looked like a happy jack-o-lantern.

It made him realize he had similar grin on his own face. "And I guess I look a bit like that too," he thought.

"I *am* happy," he said. "I love it here more than anywhere else in the world, Mimi, I mean ma'am."

Mimi Kinnell let out a deep laugh that Travis felt in his bones. She grabbed him and gave him a hug so hard that he heard his back crack. Then she held him out at arm's length.

"Partner," she said, "you are one good kid. And you can call me anything you like. You hear me?"

Travis nodded.

She held out a paper bag to him. "Picked this up at that last stop. Figured you might need a little fuel for this last leg of your journey."

Travis looked inside. There was an apple, a banana, several candy bars, and three packets of beef jerky.

He looked up at Mimi and took a deep breath. Once again someone had been so kind to him, kinder than he felt he deserved. That lump was back in his throat again.

"Thank you," he managed to whisper.

"You are more than welcome, Travis." Mimi grinned again. "Your grandparents are sure as shootin' gonna be happy to see you. It's gonna to be like the sun comin' up for them."

They'd come a short way off I-95 to a crossroad Travis knew. From there he could hike to his grandparents' cabin. It was only twenty miles. After the thousands of miles he'd come, twenty miles was nothing.

He waved goodbye as Mimi leaned out the window of the semi. She blew her air horn as she pulled out—seven blasts of it.

WHONK WHONK

WHONK WHONK WHONK

WHONK WHONK

Travis watched until she rounded a curve and went out of sight. He shifted his pack up on his back and stepped onto the logging trail that led into the forest. At first he walked, but then, after only a few hundred yards, he began to run.

His Grandparents' Cabin

As Travis ran, the sounds of his feet striking the earth made him think of a drum— like the drum at the Passamaquoddy Ceremonial Days. His grandparents had taken him there.

"Know your heritage," Grandma Kailin had said. "It's there in the songs, even the simplest ones. They always greet you and greet everything else that lives."

Travis could smell the trees, the moist earth under his feet, and other scents on the wind that were so familiar, even if he couldn't identify them exactly. There were no sounds of cars, or people, or anything except the Maine woods. He hadn't realized how much he'd missed being in the forest. He knew it wasn't peaceful in the sense that everything around him was kind and gentle, like one of those silly cartoon movies. There were birds and animals that ate each other. Even the trees and plants competed with each other as much as they cooperated. You had to be careful in the woods or you could get injured or even die. But that was all right. There was a difference here that he'd missed. Unlike the human-made world, where everything was being used and used up, here things were always in a sort of balance. Whatever lived here eventually fed other life. That was what his grandfather had told him and had shown him.

Once he and Grampa Tomah found a deer antler on the trail behind their cabin.

"Don't see that often," Grampa Tomah had said. "Deer antlers are like candy for mice and shrews. The antlers contain minerals that keep them healthy. Come back in a week and that'll

all be gone. Unless you want to take it as a
souvenir."

Travis had shaken his head.

"Good," Grampa Tomah had replied.

They'd left the deer antler where they had
found it.

Travis paused on a ridgetop where he could
look out over the forest. He could see smoke rising
to the south. Probably from a paper mill. There'd
been just a hint of that boiled-cabbage smell in
the air when he had left the road. But that and
the vapor trails of jet planes high above were the
only signs of human beings, other than the old log
road he was following. He sat on a thick cushion
of moss with his back against a cedar stump and
ate a couple of the candy bars, the apple, and
the banana. He folded the candy wrappers and
put them in the bottom of his pack. He left the
apple core and banana peel on top of a big rock,
knowing they would soon be found and eaten.

He could have made a fire using his kit, but
there was no need for that on this warm day.
A fire would be good after the sun went down.
The temperature could drop fifty degrees or
more this time of year. But by then he would
be in the cabin with his grandparents.

It was late afternoon when Travis reached the
place where he could look down from the trail

and see the cabin. There was a clearing around it and a garden with a fence to keep out the deer. It looked as it always did, and it made his heart swell to see it.

"I just hope they'll be happy to see me," Travis thought.

Then he began to notice things that looked strange.

In front of the cabin were the boxes Grandma Kailin had always used to plant petunias. But there weren't any flowers in them. To the left side of the building was the shed his grandfather had built from logs and rough lumber. The door to the shed was open, and the old pickup truck that they drove was gone.

Travis walked down the hill.

"Hello?" he called out as he neared the house. No one answered or opened the front door. "Hello," he said again. "Nmahom? Nokomis?" he called, using some of the few words he knew in their language. "Grandfather? Grandmother? It's me, Travis."

The door was ajar. He heard sounds coming from inside. But then it grew quiet.

Travis started up the wooden stairs, almost falling as the second step gave way under his weight. It was cracked in the middle and about to break in half. Why had his grandfather not fixed that step? He had always kept up with any repairs that needed to be done.

Travis was on the porch now, the partly open door in front of him. He reached out a hand and pushed the door open wider. It was much darker in the cabin than outside. He could barely see a shadowy shape bent over, like someone who has fallen on his hands and knees.

"Are you all right?" Travis asked, his voice filled with concern.

He was answered by a growl as the shadowy shape stood up from the sugar bowl it had been licking. It was a huge black bear.

"AAAARRROWWW!" it roared, and then charged straight at him.

Gone

Travis threw himself backward and to the side. He felt the bear brush past him as he rolled over one shoulder, the way he'd been taught by Master Kwan. The roll took him off the porch. He ended up on his feet just in time to see the bear disappearing into the forest. For a while Travis heard the sounds of its feet crashing through the brush and the huff! huff! huff! of its breath. Then everything was quiet except for the pounding of his heart.

What his grandfather had taught him was true. A black bear cornered by a person will charge. However, what it wants most is just to escape. But if you don't move out of its way, you could get hurt. Travis remembered a story in the news a year ago. A teenage boy in Canada had been killed when the boy surprised a black bear while it was looking for food in a camp.

Travis went back into the cabin, shut the door behind him, and latched it. Apparently it had not been closed all the way and the bear had been able to push it open.

He searched the small building, afraid of what he might find. Perhaps someone's body or—like in a movie—the signs of a struggle. All he found was empty rooms. There was no sign of anyone anywhere, including in the small room where he used to sleep when he visited. The guest bed was still there, all made up with a star quilt over the sheets.

His grandparents' room was just as empty. Grampa Tomah's pack basket and Grandma Kailin's old suitcase were gone. So were their few clothes and the toiletries from their bathroom. His grandfather's hunting rifle and fishing tackle were not in their usual places, nor were his grandmother's basket-making tools. Either they'd packed up their possessions or someone had done it for them. But where had they gone?

Travis shook his head. There was no way he could figure that out now. The sun was going down and the temperature was dropping. He was exhausted and starting to feel chilled in the dark, cold cabin. There was a pile of wood and a box of kindling next to the fireplace, as well as several candles on the mantle. He didn't see any matches, but that wasn't a problem.

He knelt on the hearthstone where Grampa Tomah had taught him the ways to make fire— from using a bow drill to touching a wad of steel wool to the top of a square battery. He took out his knife to make a pile of wood shavings and built a little tipi of sticks over the curls of dry wood. Then he removed the flint-and-steel strike from his fire-making kit. It took him only two tries to strike a spark into the shavings. He leaned close, blowing gently into the pile as first smoke and then flames rose. He added more wood and soon had a warm, roaring fire going. Then, using a burning stick from the fire, he lit two of the candles.

With one hand cupped around the flame, he went back into the kitchen. He found the cup he'd always used on a high shelf. A pitcher half filled with water stood by the pump over the sink. He poured some of the water into the pump to prime it as he worked the handle. Cool, clear water began to flow into the sink. He rinsed his cup and then filled it.

Water from a pump carries the blessing of the earth. That was how Grandma Kailin put it.

Travis lifted the cup. "Thank you," he said. Then he drank deeply.

There were a few spoons and forks in the dish drainer and some cans of beef stew in the cupboard over the sink. Travis took down one of the cans. He hefted it in his hand, then cut open the lid and took the can back to the fireplace. He placed it close enough to the fire to heat it. When bubbles began to appear in the top of the stew, he used two sticks to slide the can back from the flame. He picked it up using an old dish towel and dipped his spoon in. It tasted heavenly.

After he'd eaten, he took the candle with him to the outhouse a few yards behind the cabin. As always, it was neater than most indoor toilets. There was a stack of his grandfather's favorite hunting and fishing magazines piled up on a shelf next to the rolls of toilet paper in plastic bags to prevent mice from using them to make nests.

Back inside, Travis built up the fire. He went into his old bedroom and pulled the star quilt over himself. Then, feeling more at home than he'd felt in years, he fell asleep.

When he woke the next morning, he made another search of the cabin. This time he looked in the two wastebaskets. Inside the ash-splint basket in his grandparents' bedroom he found the answer—a brochure about a place called Deer Meadows.

"ASSISTED LIVING FOR ELDERS" it read. "Long-term residence for those who wish to spend their golden years in a friendly, worry-free setting."

Travis took note of the address and then shoved the brochure into his backpack. He went outside, made sure the door was shut securely, faced south, and started running.

The sun was in the middle of the sky by the time he reached the place. It was at the edge of the city, on a hilltop in a quiet residential area. There was a really big meadow around the sprawling new three-story building. Bees buzzed through the beds of flowers planted all along the curving driveway. Travis heard a cardinal calling from the old maple trees at the edge of the meadow. He liked the way Deer Meadows had been built so that it wasn't totally separated from nature, even though he did not like the idea of his grandparents being stuck in such a place.

"ENTER" read the sign over the front door. But it was locked.

Travis pressed the button next to the door.

"Yes?" a woman's efficient voice answered from the speaker above the button.

"I think my grandparents may be here, ma'am."

"Name?"

"Travis. Travis Hawk."

A metallic click came from the door. Travis pushed it open and went inside. An African-American woman in a white uniform was sitting at the desk in front of him. She smiled and gestured for him to approach. The name tag on her coat read "Ms. Hurston, RN."

"Travis Hawk?" Ms. Hurston asked.

"Yes, ma'am. That's me."

"Very good," she said, looking at a paper on the desk in front of her. "Expected, I see. But I do require some form of picture identification. For security reasons, you understand."

"Of course, ma'am," Travis said, swinging his backpack around to the front. He pulled out his driver's license. "Will this do?"

Ms. Hurston studied the license, then jotted something down, and handed it back to him along with a clip-on tag with the word "VISITOR" printed on it. "You're all set, young man. Just keep this tag in plain sight." She looked down at another sheet of paper on her neatly kept desk.

"Lunch," she said. "Excellent. As a guest of your relatives, you're entitled to dine with them for free."

As she spoke those words, Travis's stomach growled. It reminded him how hungry he was. The last thing he'd eaten was the stew from the night before. He was as hungry as the bear that had bowled him over.

Ms. Hurston raised an eyebrow. Then she laughed out loud, and the businesslike look on her face turned into a warm smile. "Hungry, are we?"

Travis smiled back. "I guess so, ma'am."

Ms. Hurston chuckled. "Then no need to dillydally. See the facility map on the wall there? They'll be in the dining hall. They should be at . . ." She consulted another paper. "Table four. That's their table. Right near the western window. I'll call ahead for them to expect you."

"Thank you, ma'am."

"Don't mention it. Now get along, Travis. Your grandparents are going to be delighted to see you."

Travis walked down the hallway to the right. He climbed a set of stairs and came out on a landing with doors open to both sides down a broader hall. Each door had the name of the resident whose apartment it was. No one seemed to be around. Probably all eating. Travis's stomach growled again.

The long hallway curved and then opened into a big room. Sun streamed in through the windows on three sides. Fifty or sixty people, most of them with snowy hair, were sitting at the tables placed all around the dining room. Travis began to walk forward. Elderly people turned to look at him as he passed. Some nodded; some said hello. Travis nodded back and said hello in turn as he tried to find the right table. It wasn't that hard to see which was which, as each table had a stand in the middle of it with a big numbered sign.

Table 21. Table 16. Table 8.

Then he saw it. It was right next to a window, just as Ms. Hurston had said. Table 4. Just two people were at that table, and one of them was standing up—a tall woman with a straight back, her long hair in a braid that hung over her left shoulder. There was a happy smile on her face, and she was holding out her arms.

"Nosis!" she said. "Grandson." She pulled him into a strong hug. "*Paakwenogwisian*. You appear new to me. We are so glad you are finally here."

"Nokomis," Travis whispered. His throat felt so choked that it was hard for him to speak. "I missed you so much."

A hand grasped his wrist.

"How about me, grandson? You miss this old broken branch, too?"

Travis looked down. It took him a moment to see clearly because his eyes were filled with mist. It was Grampa Tomah, all right. But why was he not standing? Then Travis saw the cane in his grandfather's left hand, the wheelchair he was sitting in, and the cast on his left foot. He also saw how small Grampa Tomah looked in that chair. He seemed so much older and thinner than Travis remembered.

His grandmother released him from her arms. Travis dropped to one knee, his hands on his grandfather's arms.

"Gramps, what happened?"

"Dumb luck," his grandfather said with a grin.

"And don't forget laziness," his grandmother added in a teasing voice. She shook her head. "How many times did I tell you to mend that back step, old man?"

Grampa Tomah reached up and took his wife's hand. "She's always right, you know."

They smiled at each other in the same way Travis remembered from the past. There was so much love between them, the kind of love Travis had not felt in his own homeless life for what seemed like ages. So many thoughts were going through his head now that he felt dizzy.

He was so glad to see his grandparents, but he was also so upset at how weak his grandfather looked. He'd made it to them, but his dream of living with them had vanished. They were now in a place where he couldn't join them. "Long-term residential care"—that meant forever. Then another thought struck him. They'd known he was coming. That had to be because his father had contacted them. Travis's heart sank. He'd come all this way, and now he was probably just going to be sent right back.

Grandma Kailin put a hand on his shoulder. He looked up at her.

"Don't worry, nosis. Here, take this."

She was holding out a cell phone. A cell phone?

Grampa Tomah chuckled. "Yup, grandson. Your grandma and me have become nowadays Indians. We are all hooked into the worldwide web. Got us that Facetime and all. Now you take that call. My boy's been worried about you."

Travis felt numb. But he took the phone. He held it up and his father's face looked back at him through the screen. Travis almost pushed the red button to end the call.

But his father held up a hand. "Trav, son," he said. "I am so sorry."

Travis had heard those words often from his father.

"You look good, Trav," Rick Hawk said. "Real good."

"Thank you, sir."

Rick Hawk shook his head. "No. No. Don't call me 'sir.' I do not deserve that. I don't even deserve to be called Dad. But I am going to try. Look! Check this out."

His father moved the phone away from his own face. He swung it around so that Travis could see the room his father was in. It was a big room with other people in it. Some of them waved. Then it stopped at a big sign on the wall that read "Drug and Alcohol Treatment Center."

His father's face came back on the screen. "I checked in here the day after you left, Trav. I figured out right away what you'd done. It was just as clear to me as why you felt you had to do it—run away from me, I mean. I thought at first about going after you." His father shook his head. "Decided not to do that. When you run, son, there's no one who can catch you. I guessed where you would be heading. And I decided there were two things I could do. The first was to trust you. The second was to accept what I'd done, what I'd become. And that is why I am here. Clean and sober since you left."

Travis nodded. He'd heard all that before too. He didn't say anything.

"Do you believe me?" Rick Hawk said. "It's okay if you don't. But I really do mean it. I am really going to try. I want you to be as proud of me as I am of you."

Travis took a deep breath. He bit his lip. "You want me to come back now?"

"What?" Rick Hawk shook his head. "You kidding me? No way, no how. You stay there with my mom and dad. They are going to need your help for a while."

Travis felt confused. "In here? But this is long-term care. I can't—"

Grandma Kailin leaned down next to his ear. "Not long-term, nosis. Just temporary. Your

grampa used to be a guide for the man who
directs this place. Pulled some strings to get us
in here just until this old coot is back on his feet
or we can find us a live-in helper." She punched
him gently on the shoulder. "You know anyone
like that?"

Rick Hawk's face split into the kind of grin
that used to be there before Travis's mom died.
"Hear that, son? If you're available, you three
can head back to their cabin right away. Seems
to me that, in the long run, that's the best place
for you to be for a while."

Travis was smiling now, a broad grin that
matched the one beaming up at him from the
phone in his palm.

"Thank you, Dad," he said. "I . . . I love you."

"I love you, too, Trav. I just hope someday
I'll be able to make you respect me again. Now
travel well and take care of yourself and your
grandparents."

His father's face vanished from the screen
into a point of light.

It was the old way of doing it, even on
something as modern as an iPhone. You never
said a long goodbye if you were an Indian. You
just wished each other a good journey and then
turned away.

Travis lifted his head and looked out the window toward the west.

"You, too, Dad," Travis whispered. Then he wrapped his arms around his grandparents.

About the Author

oseph Bruchac is a traditional storyteller and the author of over 120 books. His work often reflects his American Indian (Abenaki) ancestry and the Adirondack region of northern New York, where he lives in the house in which he was raised by his grandparents.

A martial arts expert, Joseph holds a fifth-degree black belt and master's rank in pentjak silat, and in 2014 he earned a purple belt in Brazilian jiu jitsu. He and his two grown sons, James and Jesse, who are also storytellers and writers, work together on projects to preserve Native culture, restore Native languages, and teach traditional Native skills and environmental awareness.

PathFinders novels offer exciting contemporary and historical stories featuring Native teens and written by Native authors. For more information, visit: NativeVoicesBooks.com

also by Joesph Bruchac

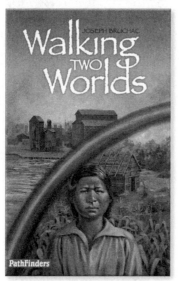

"*Through brief chapters and vivid descriptions, Bruchac, who is of partial Abenaki descent, offers a full-bodied portrait of a dedicated young man holding on to the traditions of his heritage while adapting to an encroaching world.*"

PUBLISHER WEEKLY REVIEWS
APRIL 2015

Walking Two Worlds
Joseph Bruchac

Paperback • 978-1-939053-10-7 • $9.95
Hardcover • 978-1-939053-13-8 • $16.95

Available from your local bookstore or directly from:
Book Publishing Company • P.O. Box 99 • Summertown, TN 38483
888-260-8458
Please include $3.95 per book for shipping and handling.